W9-ADJ-310

Marsh Music

By Marianne Berkes

Illustrated by
Robert Noreika

M Millbrook Press • Minneapolis

To my daughter, Melissa.
And in joyful memory of my parents,
Anne & Harry Staffhorst,
who filled my life with many songs.
—MB

To Sarah, Chris, and my father.
—RN

Millbrook Press
A division of Lerner Publishing Group
241 First Avenue North
Minneapolis, MN 55401 USA

Website address: www.lernerbooks.com

Library of Congress Cataloging-in-Publication Data
Berkes, Marianne.
Marsh music/by Marianne Berkes;
illustrated by Robert Noreika.
p. cm.
Summary: During the night, the marsh comes alive
with the singing of all kinds of frogs, from spring peepers
and wood frogs to leopard and pig frogs.
ISBN 0-7613-1850-X (lib. bdg.)
[1. Frogs—Fiction. 2. Animal sounds—Fiction. 3. Stories in rhyme.]
I.Noreika, Robert, ill. II. Title.
PZ8.3. B4557 2000
[E]—dc21   99-051641

Manufactured in the United States of America
4 5 6 7 8 9 – DP – 10 09 08 07 06 05

"Frogs do for the night
what birds do for the day;
they give it a voice.
And the voice is
a varied and stirring one
that ought to be better known."

—Dr. Archie Carr,
The Everglades

The rain has stopped.
Night is coming.
The pond awakes with
quiet humming.

Maestro frog hops to the mound
As night begins to fill with sound.

Peepers peep *pe-ep*, *peep*, *peep*.
They have had a good day's sleep!

Spring
peepers

Chorus frogs are hard to see.
Hear them chirping *do re mi.*

Then the other frogs come in.
Soon the concert will begin.

Chorus frogs

Fireflies light up the stage
as the maestro turns the page

Maestro raises his baton.
Now it's time to carry on.

The woodwinds whistle a l o n g,
sweet trill.

The strings go
twang,
   twang,
      twang.

The horns bleat loudly
whaaa,
   whaaa,
      whaaa,

Percussions snap
and bang.

Green
frogs

Wood
frogs

American
toads

Narrow-
mouthed
toads

Maestro starts out kind of slow.
They're playing in "adagio."

Then he motions to the bass.
The tempo starts to change.
They're playing at a faster pace
And in a higher range.

Pig
frogs

Green
tree
frogs

Longer notes. Shorter notes.
Listen to the quarter notes.

Woink-woink-woink
Woink-woink-woink
Three-quarter time.

Gronk-gronk-gronk
Gronk-gronk-gronk
Music sublime.

Two leopard frogs
leap through the air.
They're dancing a ballet.

Leopard
frogs

They pirouette on lily pads
And then they swim away.

Barking
tree
frog

A tree frog glides onto a frond
As sounds keep rising from the pond.

"Aarf, aarf," he calls down from the tree
And joins the outdoor symphony.

Stars are twinkling to the tune
As they dance around the moon.

The orchestra plays "moderato."
Maestro motions "animato."

Faster, louder, wondrous sounds.
Music of the night abounds!

There is a pause—then wild applause.
Bravo! Encore! We want some more!"

But now it's dawn.
The stars are gone.
Maestro puts down his baton.

That's all my friends.
It's time to go.
Tonight there'll be
another show.

The marsh is quiet.
No more ringing.
But wait, I think
I hear some singing!

The day's awake. Now it's morning.
A melody is heard!
Can't be frogs, 'cause they're asleep.
I think I hear . . .

. . . a bird!

Glossary
of Musical Terms

Adagio　　　　slowly

Animato　　　　to play with vigor

Baton　　　　a slender stick the leader uses to direct the orchestra.

Horns　　　　the brass section of the orchestra. Brass instruments are: trumpets, French horns, trombones, and tubas.

Maestro　　　　conductor or teacher of music

Moderato　　　　to play with moderation of tempo

Percussion　　　　Percussion instruments are: drums, cymbals, bells, triangles, harp, and piano.

Pirouette　　　　a whirling around on one foot or the point of a toe, especially in ballet

Quarter note　　　　a musical note with the time value of one quarter of a whole note

Strings　　　　the largest section of the orchestra. String instruments are: violins, violas, cellos, double basses.

Symphony　　　　consonance of sounds: a concert

Tempo　　　　the speed at which a musical composition is performed

Three-quarter time　　　　usually a waltz where the accent is on the first beat

Woodwinds　　　　Woodwind instruments are: flutes, clarinets, oboes and bassoon.

The Cast

"Maestro" Bullfrog (3½ to 8 inches/9 to 20 cm) North America's largest frog species, bullfrogs are yellowish green to black, sometimes mottled with dark spots. Bullfrogs call a deep, resonant "jug-o-rum" that can be heard for long distances. They are strictly aquatic and can be found in lakes and ponds.

Spring Peepers (¾ to 1⅜ inches/1.9 to 3.5 cm) are small, slender brown or olive-gray frogs with pointed heads. They breed in swamps and live in low bushes and plants. When they sing in full chorus, their sharp, high-pitched series of whistles and trills, pe-ep, pe-ep, pe-ep, can be deafening!

Chorus Frogs (¾ to 1⅜ inches/1.9 to 3.5 cm) are gray with dark spots and often blend in with their surroundings. They have slim bodies and pointed snouts, and sound like a comb clicking. The upland chorus frog has a "vibrating" chirp, while the ornate chorus frog has a clear long chirp.

American Toads (2 to 4⅜ inches/5 to 11 cm) Short and fat in body, toads come in a variety of color, usually brown, gray, olive, or red with various-sized warts. The American toad's song sounds like a sweet trilling whistle. It is a sustained trill that sounds like "bu-rr-r-r."

Green Frogs (2 to 4 inches/5 to 10 cm) live in swamps and ponds in the eastern United States. They are usually greenish brown with a bright green mask from the tympanum (eardrum) toward the jaw. Their call sounds like the plucking of a string bass or the twang of a rubber band slightly stretched over an open box.

Narrow-mouthed Toads ($^7/_8$ to $1^1/_2$ inches/2.2 to 3.8 cm) are dark-colored with small heads and pointed snouts. This tiny toad's loud "whaaa" sounds like a bleating sheep. Nocturnal, a lover of rain and moist areas, the narrow-mouthed toad calls from shallow water with rear feet submerged and forefeet planted on the bank.

Wood Frogs ($1^1/_2$ to $3^1/_4$ inches/3.5 to 8.3 cm) are often a bright metallic copper color with dark masks over their eyes. They live in woodlands, except when they go to and from marshes to breed. Vocalizing males make short, raspy, ducklike sounds: a sharp, snappy, clack— 2, 4, or 6 notes in succession.

Pig Frogs ($3^1/_4$ to 6 inches/8 to 15 cm) are similar to bullfrogs and are brownish olive to gray with a creamy-colored underside netted with a brownish pattern. The tops of their heads are dark green. Strictly aquatic, pig frogs call from lily pads and sound like pigs grunting: woink, woink, woink.

Green Tree Frogs ($1^1/_2$ to $2^1/_2$ inches/3.5 to 6 cm) are especially active on damp or rainy evenings and are easily seen around the edges of ponds and lakes, particularly among cattails. Slender and smooth, the beautiful bright-green tree frog has a light stripe along its upper jaw and side. Its call is: gronk, gronk, gronk.

Leopard Frogs (2 to 4 inches/5 to 10 cm) are slender and smooth skinned. They vary in color from light brown to dark green with leopardlike brown spots. Found around any body of water, their unusually long hind legs allow them to launch into the air, soaring great distances. The leopard frog's call is long and low, interspersed with clucking grunts.

Barking Tree Frogs (2 to $2^3/_4$ inches/5 to 7 cm) This is our largest native tree frog, green to greenish brown, its back covered with round brown spots. Quite pudgy in build and one of the most colorful tree frogs, a breeding chorus of barking tree frogs sounds like dogs barking.

About the Author and Illustrator

Marianne Berkes was an early childhood educator and also directed children's theater in Pawling, New York, before moving to Florida where she is a children's librarian. "Miss Marianne," as she is known to the children in the Palm Beach County Library System, enjoys telling stories about frogs and nature. She lives in Hobe Sound with her husband, Roger. The cacophony of sounds she often hears from the pond in back of their home served as the inspiration for this, her first book.

This is the third book for artist Robert Noreika, following his work in *A Moon for Seasons* and *Exploring Mountain Habits.* An award-winning member of the Connecticut Watercolor Society and the Salmagundi Club in New York City, Noreika also teaches classes throughout the New England region. He enjoys long treks in the woods with his family. Noreika and his wife have one daughter; they live in Rocky Hill, Connecticut.

Farm Flu

WRITTEN BY Teresa Bateman

ILLUSTRATED BY Nadine Bernard Westcott

Albert Whitman & Company
Morton Grove, Illinois

Library of Congress Cataloging-in-Publication Data

Bateman, Teresa.

Farm flu / by Teresa Bateman ; illustrated by Nadine Bernard Westcott.

p. cm.

Summary: When the farm animals seem to catch the flu one after another,

a young boy does his best to take care of them.

ISBN 0-8075-2274-0 (hardcover)

[1. Influenza—Fiction. 2. Domestic animals—Fiction. 3. Stories in rhyme.]

I. Westcott, Nadine Bernard, ill. II. Title.

PZ8.3.W4998 Far 2000

[E]—dc21

00-008158

Text copyright © 2001 by Teresa Bateman.

Illustrations copyright © 2001 by Nadine Bernard Westcott.

Published in 2001 by Albert Whitman & Company,

6340 Oakton Street, Morton Grove, Illinois 60053-2723.

Published simultaneously in Canada by Fitzhenry & Whiteside, Markham, Ontario.

Printed in the United States of America.

10 9 8 7 6

The design is by Scott Piehl.

For Steven, Joanna, and Maren,
who know just what their mom would do.
— T. B.

For Sarah, with love.
— N. B. W.

My mom's a farmer,
so am I.
We work the farm
through wet and dry.

But it was likely just as well
that Mom was out of town a spell
when, marching through the morning dew,
I heard the milk cow moo,

"Ka-Chooo!"

"Poor thing," I said,
"you've got the flu!"

I'd never helped a sickly cow.
(I just know how to milk and plow.)

But I knew what my mom would do
if it were me who had the flu.

I tucked the Guernsey into bed
with tissues for her stuffy head.

I brought her hot alfalfa tea

and fluffed her pillows hourly.

The next day I was up at dawn.
(The Guernsey cow kept snoring on.)

I heard a "cock-a-doodle-doo," and then the chickens clucked,

"Ka-Chooo!"

I knew just what my mom would do
if it were me who had the flu.

The TV room became a coop!
I brought them bowls of barley soup.

The barnyard called with chores to do,
but then the piglets squealed,

"Ka-Chooo!"

I knew just what my mom would do
if it were me who had the flu.

I popped the piglets in the tub
and gave them all a belly rub.

I knew just what my mom would do
if it were me who had the flu.

They changed the channel, asked for snacks—
said popcorn helped them to relax.
They got out chess and checkers, too,

and then the donkey brayed,

"Ka-Chooo!"

More popcorn, please!

I knew just what my mom would do
if it were me who had the flu.

Reclining on the back porch swing,
he asked for some of everything.

And then a wild and woolly crew
arrived and loudly ba-a-a-ed,

"Ka-Chooo!"

Ka-Chooo!

Ka-Chooo!

CARDS

I knew just what my mom would do
if it were me who had the flu.

The attic had a little room;
I cleaned it up with mop and broom
and settled all my woolly guests

while urging them
to get some rest.

That night I didn't get much sleep.
(My room was underneath the sheep.)
The house was filled with cluck, oink, moo.
How odd they all should catch the flu!

The next day I arose and yawned.
The house was still as morning dawned.
I stopped.
I listened.
No Ka-choo!

I knew just what my mom would do.

"Too sick to be outside, I see.
Then you're too sick to watch TV!
No toys, no games, just stay in bed.
No popcorn—
you'll have mush instead!"

A miracle—they all were cured!
They hurried out without a word
and galloped to the barn with glee—
recuperating magically.

I followed, but my steps were slow.
I felt like half-baked sourdough.
Relieved the end was now in view,
I stumbled,
blinked,
and sneezed,

They quickly treated me for flu—
exactly as my mom would do.